The Twelve Days of Christmas

HILARY KNIGHT'S
The Twelve Days of Christmas

Simon & Schuster Books for Young Readers
New York   London   Toronto   Sydney   Singapore

SIMON & SCHUSTER BOOKS FOR YOUNG READERS
An imprint of Simon & Schuster Children's Publishing Division
1230 Avenue of the Americas, New York, New York 10020
Copyright © 1981, 2001 by Hilary Knight
Revised format edition, 2001
All rights reserved including the right of reproduction in whole or in part in any form.
SIMON & SCHUSTER BOOKS FOR YOUNG READERS is a trademark of Simon & Schuster.
2 4 6 8 10 9 7 5 3 1
The Library of Congress has cataloged a previous edition as follows:
Twelve days of Christmas (English folk song) Hilary Knight's the twelve days of Christmas.
Summary: More and more gifts arrive from a young bear's true love on each of the twelve days of Christmas.
[1. Folk songs, English. 2. Christmas music] I. Knight, Hilary. II. Title
PZ8.3.T8517 1981   784.4'05   81-2599
ISBN 0-689-83547-7

for
Katharine
and
Clayton

Joey
&
Betsey

Benjamin
&
Bedelia

On the 1st day of Christmas
my true love gave to me:
A partridge in a pear tree.

On the 2nd day of Christmas
my true love gave to me:
Two turtle doves,
And a partridge in a pear tree.

On the 3rd day of Christmas
my true love gave to me:
Three French hens,
Two turtle doves,
And a partridge in a pear tree.

On the 4th day of Christmas
my true love gave to me:
Four calling birds,
Three French hens,
Two turtle doves,
And a partridge in a pear tree.

On the 5th day of Christmas
my true love gave to me:

Five gold rings,
Four calling birds,
Three french hens,
Two turtle doves,
And a partridge in a pear tree.

On the 6th day of Christmas
my true love gave to me:

Six geese a-laying,
Five gold rings,
Four calling birds,
Three French hens,
Two turtle doves,
And a partridge in a pear tree.

On the 7th day of Christmas
my true love gave to me:
Seven swans a-swimming,
Six geese a-laying,
Five gold rings,
Four calling birds,
Three French hens,
Two turtle doves,
And a partridge in a pear tree.

On the 8th day of Christmas
my true love gave to me:
Eight maids a-milking,
Seven swans a-swimming,
Six geese a-laying,
Five gold rings,
Four calling birds,
Three French hens,
Two turtle doves,
And a partridge in a pear tree.

On the 9th day of Christmas
my true love gave to me:
Nine drummers drumming,
Eight maids a-milking,
Seven swans a-swimming,
Six geese a-laying,
Five gold rings,
Four calling birds,
Three French hens,
Two turtle doves,
And a partridge in a pear tree.

On the 10th day of Christmas
my true love gave to me:
Ten fiddlers fiddling,
Nine drummers drumming,
Eight maids a-milking,
Seven swans a-swimming,
Six geese a-laying,
Five gold rings,
Four calling birds,
Three french hens,
Two turtle doves,
And a partridge in a pear tree.

On the 11th day of Christmas
my true love gave to me:
Eleven ladies dancing,
Ten fiddlers fiddling,
Nine drummers drumming,
Eight maids a-milking,
Seven swans a-swimming,
Six geese a-laying,
Five gold rings,
Four calling birds,
Three French hens,
Two turtle doves,
And a partridge in a pear tree.

On the 12th day of Christmas
my true love gave to me:
Twelve lords a-leaping,
Eleven ladies dancing,
Ten fiddlers fiddling,
Nine drummers drumming,
Eight maids a-milking,
Seven swans a-swimming,
Six geese a-laying,
Five gold rings,
Four calling birds,
Three French hens,
Two turtle doves,
And a partridge in a pear tree.

HENNY 30!
ANNIE · BETTE
CLAUDETTE
DELPHINE · ELSA ·
FANNY · GINETTE
HÉLÈNE · INEZ ·
JACQUELINE ·
KITTI · LILI · MIMI ·
MIRABELLE · MARGOT ·
NANA · NINA · OLAMPE ·
PAULETTE ·
QUIN-QUIN ·
RENNÉE · SILVIE · SIMONE ·
TRINA · URSULA · VERE · WINNIE
MADAME X · YVETTE · ZIZI!

PEAR JAM

JELLY

The text illustrations for this book were created in 1980 and reseparated in 2001 for this edition.

Endpaper illustrations were created in 2000.

The illustrations were rendered in watercolor and colored pencil.

Jacket and text hand-lettering by Hilary Knight

Book design by Jennifer Reyes and Hilary Knight

Printed in the United States of America